Dear Parent:
Your child's love of reading starts here!

Every child learns to read in a different way and at his or her own speed. Some go back and forth between reading levels and read favorite books again and again. Others read through each level in order. You can help your young reader improve and become more confident by encouraging his or her own interests and abilities. From books your child reads with you to the first books he or she reads alone, there are I Can Read Books for every stage of reading:

SHARED READING
Basic language, word repetition, and whimsical illustrations, ideal for sharing with your emergent reader

BEGINNING READING
Short sentences, familiar words, and simple concepts for children eager to read on their own

READING WITH HELP
Engaging stories, longer sentences, and language play for developing readers

READING ALONE
Complex plots, challenging vocabulary, and high-interest topics for the independent reader

ADVANCED READING
Short paragraphs, chapters, and exciting themes for the perfect bridge to chapter books

I Can Read Books have introduced children to the joy of reading since 1957. Featuring award-winning authors and illustrators and a fabulous cast of beloved characters, I Can Read Books set the standard for beginning readers.

A lifetime of discovery begins with the magical words "I Can Read!"

Visit www.icanread.com for information on enriching your child's reading experience.

EXPLORING THE
GREAT OUTDOORS

BY MERCER MAYER

HARPER
An Imprint of HarperCollinsPublishers

To Wesley and Natalie Clark,
Jaxon McFarland and family

I Can Read Book® is a trademark of HarperCollins Publishers.

Little Critter: Exploring the Great Outdoors
Copyright © 2019 by Mercer Mayer. All rights reserved. LITTLE CRITTER, MERCER MAYER'S LITTLE CRITTER and
MERCER MAYER'S LITTLE CRITTER and logo are registered trademarks of Orchard House Licensing Company. All rights
reserved. Manufactured in U.S.A. No part of this book may be used or reproduced in any manner whatsoever without written
permission except in the case of brief quotations embodied in critical articles and reviews. For information address HarperCollins
Children's Books, a division of HarperCollins Publishers, 195 Broadway, New York, NY 10007.
www.icanread.com

Library of Congress Control Number: 2017943573
ISBN 978-0-06-243145-5 (trade bdg.) — ISBN 978-0-06-243144-8 (pbk.)

20 21 22   LSCC   10 9   ❖   First Edition

A Big Tuna Trading Company, LLC/J. R. Sansevere Book
www.littlecritter.com

My class goes on a hike.

We ride a school bus.

We stop at the Critterville State Park.

A forest ranger greets us.

He will be our guide.

He shows us the rules of the forest.

I put on my ranger hat.

Now I am ready.

THE PARK RULES
1. Stay on the path.
2. If you see a snake,
   do not touch.
3. If you see a bear,
   do not run.
4. If you see a mama
   bear with a cub,
   walk away quickly
   and quietly.

IF YOU ARE EATEN BY A BEAR,
WE ARE NOT RESPONSIBLE

PUT TRASH HERE

At the park store

we buy healthy snacks for the trail.

Then off we go.

We hike and hike.

We walk and walk.

Gator falls down.

He needs a bandage.

Next we cross a rope bridge.

Oops! The ranger falls in.

He is very unhappy.

I am happy to see a frog.

We meet a little bear cub.

"We need to go before the mama shows up," says the ranger.

We walk very fast,

but the bear cub follows us.

Oh no! The mama bear shows up.

The bear cub runs to the mama.

She is happy.

They walk away.

We walk the other way.

But I am not happy.

I lost my ranger hat.

We see a skunk in the path,

but we stay very still.

Timothy climbs a tree

and can't get down.

Miss Kitty saves the day.

The ranger points to the ranger tower.
He wants us to climb to the top
and see where he works.

"I think we are too tired
to climb the tower today."
Miss Kitty says.

We have snacks.

Timothy lost his snack.

Everyone shares.

There are too many ants.

We leave quickly.

Ants are crawling everywhere.

We find leaves for a scrapbook.

"No!" says the ranger.

"That is poison ivy."

It is time to go.

I find my park ranger hat.

There are holes in it.

We hike to the bus.

The last hill is the hardest.

The ranger waves goodbye.

We drive away.

Exploring the great outdoors was a lot of fun. But now we are tired.

Maybe next time we can climb

the ranger tower

to see the view.

More Little Critter® I CAN READ!™ books
for you to love:

I Can Read!™

Little Critter® and his classmates take a field trip to the state park. There's so much to see and explore, and plenty of big surprises in the great outdoors!

My First ... emergent readers

1 Simple sentences for eager new readers

2 High-interest stories for developing readers

3 Complex plots for confident readers

4 The perfect bridge to chapter books

For more information about the I Can Read Book® series, see inside!

HARPER
An Imprint of HarperCollinsPublishers
www.icanread.com
Cover art © 2019 by Mercer Mayer
All rights reserved.
www.littlecritter.com

harpercollinschildrens.com

USA $4.99 / $5.99 CAN
ISBN 978-0-06-243144-8

5 0499

9 780062 431448

GUIDED READING LEVEL **H**

DBW829331